Wings Unfurled

Cover illustration by Annabelle Windsor.

ISBN:
Imprint: Independently published, Amazon

First printed in: United Kingdom
First Edition, 2023

@libbyjenner.poetry

Wings Unfurled

Wings Unfurled

By Libby Jenner
Illustrated by Annabelle Windsor

Wings Unfurled

A NOTE FROM THE AUTHOR

The garden described in *don't be shy, dearest butterfly* seems so whimsical and surreal because it was her place of rest away from reality: it protected her when she felt the absence of safety in her waking life. But *Wings Unfurled* explores more growing pains, discomfort, and vulnerability, as I have soared into my next era of writing: I'm trying to compose work outside of my own inner garden.

It is a privilege to age and to write about it, so I am both intrigued, eager, and terrified to learn more about the versions of myself that I will grow into. I will always have space to learn, so this book is by no means the final book in my own journey.

Wings Unfurled dips into the changes that have twisted my path and discoveries I've stumbled over since being submerged into adulthood. It is not extensive, as there's still much to live through, but the illustrious poems describe moments that I have experienced thus far.

You may read this book and find that the sequences of poems are disjointed with their style and purpose, but this is both to intentionally reflect how chaotic adulthood has felt and to give me space to explore a plethora of topics under each chapter.

I hope that you can find solace in the journey of the protagonist and grow alongside her. This character is a representation of my own experiences, but she also encompasses all that I wish to become: complicated,

Libby Jenner

loved, self-assured, powerful, and unapologetically emotional.

I hope to be as gentle with myself as my protagonist is with her own journey, and I hope you are gentle with yourself, too.

Libby Jenner

CONTENTS

Wings Unfurled

Libby Jenner

Wings Unfurled

Libby Jenner

I walked into the garden when I was a child: I desperately needed a safe space to understand my emotions and reclaim the love that was stolen from me, but I am ready to grow beyond this surreal place. When the breeze whispered that the peridot door was ready to be opened, I knew that I wanted to unveil what new journey was beyond it.

Libby Jenner

CHAPTER ONE

Wings Unfurled

Moments from the last few years in my garden of healing brush over my vision as I stand in front of the peridot door that had, until now, remained sealed. I don't want to leave my younger self behind, but I must show her that we can keep growing and evolving despite the pain we may experience. And I also need a new story for myself, and to set the foundations for whoever I grow into, next.

After a deep intake of breath and a steady count to three, I reach out for the handle and twist. With a slight pull it opens with a soft *whoosh*. My stomach clenches and my legs waver as I take a couple steps into darkness. I consider closing the door and walking back to my garden but, as if sensing my indecision, four glowing orbs appear: orange, green, purple, and blue. An invitation of soft thrums ripple across the pool of darkness that their light swims in, and it gives me the reassurance to continue walking. The doors creaks behind me and I turn to see my garden home disappear: my decision sealed just as the peridot door was and is, again, now. Another gentle thrum dapples, and I walk closer to the glowing orbs to see that they are, in fact, four butterflies. The blue butterfly has wings of cascading water, the orange has flickering flames of ochre and topaz, the green has viridian ferns laced over weavings of roots, and the purple butterfly hovers gently as its lilac cloud wings float in a gentle breeze that I'm yet to feel on my skin.

"We are The Elemental Butterflies," says a voice that trickles like an eager stream, "we have watched you grow both in your garden and before then, and we are here to support you with what is next…"

The fern winged butterfly soars towards me, and I hesitantly give her my extended arm to land on. She has a touch resembling the softness of flower petals, which eases me. "I am The Earth Butterfly, my sisters are keepers of water, fire, and air. It is a pleasure to finally meet you."

The heat of The Fire Butterfly creeps over my skin as she circles me in observation, "How are you feeling? Excited? Nervous? Are you ready? You look a little tense. So shall we get started?" I can't tell whether my heart or her wings are beating faster.

"Let's just... let our newly winged friend think for a moment, this is probably very overwhelming for her." The Air Butterfly whispers gently. Her cloud wings fade from sunset lilacs to blushing dawns, and I focus on her calming trance to clear my mind and ease the tightness in my chest.

"So," I begin, "thank you for offering to support me with where I am going next, it's nice to not feel alone..." I pause for a moment as I recall what The Air Butterfly called me, "...winged friend... winged... oh my gosh WINGS!" I startle The Elemental Butterflies into a multicoloured blur as I stand abruptly and twist my body around to try and look at my back. Glassy wings, folded like scrolls, protrude from the middle of my spine, and I scoff in disbelief. "How did I get WINGS? This is not what I was expecting.... I mean I don't know *what* I was expecting in the first place but *this*..."

The Water Butterfly flies into my eyeline, and her voice is cool against my flushed cheeks, "I understand this is intense for you. This change is abrupt. Take your time, and when you are ready, we can take the next step together, okay?"

I nod and smile at her graciously. The Elemental Butterflies hover at each side of me: I am illuminated in their auras as I contemplate the difficulties that this new transformation will bring.

Wings Unfurled

"I'm ready. I want to see how my wings unfurl."

Libby Jenner

Wings Unfurled

CHAPTER TWO

I ebb and flow like a stream. Sometimes the meanders are tighter than others, sometimes the tributaries lead me to a new part of myself to explore, and other times I am floating gently through my existence.

These poems are for when my emotions have felt like both a gentle stream and a thrashing storm. And when my empowerment has felt like a colossal wave.

It is also for the moments I have concocted cyclones.

My wings are fins.

A message from the water butterfly:

When you are with me, we explore your emotions and how they store in your body both presently and overtime. I will hold your hand as memories wash onto shore and remain close as each new wave passes.

I am here to guide you along your streams and scream downpours for your thunderous storms. You have spent too many years sinking; it is time to float up to the surface and break through what has kept you under.

Wings Unfurled

Changing the Water in My Body

lifted from a dusted corner
and placed in the sun's gaze, warmer,

an embellished vase woven with chips;
a pristine shine swathes each dip,

fresh water flows into its chest;
quartz clear from the angels, blessed,

silently, it stands mounted;
many sundown's have been counted,

but glassy this vase of water has stayed
and now follows a floral array,

rusted mango and burnt amber;
forest ferns that try to clamber,

the water takes an olive hue;
stems begin rotting out of view,

from the surface fauna blooms
despite the murky impending doom,

growth shows the wonder in life itself
for who wants to stay stuck on a shelf?

but the process is not linear to arrange;
care is needed so the water is changed.

Libby Jenner

New Beginnings in the Sunrise

Poetry flows out of the colours in the sunset
and rests upon the silk cloth waves
that the horizon gushes teal and saffron over.
Ethereal phrases dip their vowels into the liquid sky and
a crest of delicacy serenades the words.

"In this moment, the words softly spoken to my body are
as gentle as these waves. I glow like the setting sun, and
I'll continue to glow through the dark.
I am more than the pretty pigments of this sunset: I am
divine, I am washed in creativity, kind threads sew my
insecurities closed, love has seeped from the slithers of
light and absorbed itself into my skin, and I accept myself
for all that I am.

I am loved.
I am creative.
I am content.
I am moving forward.
I am waiting for new beginnings in the sunrise."

And then she sets, sleeping into dusk
as the moon begins her night shift.
The waves continue to be gentle,
forever flowing,
because they have their moon to cast
a glittering sheen on their ebbing darkness.

Wings Unfurled

Thunder is Brewing in My Chest

I am not going to wait
for your storm to pass,
wait in your rain and thunderous temper;
soaked to the bone with the blood
of who I was;
electrified with bolts of your criticism;
my insides scorched by your words.

When your storm hits
I will scream so loud that your tempest cowers at my feet.
I'll stroke the lightening with my hands
and let it nestle around my hair:
it'll comb through the wind swept strands
and hold them from my eyes
as I run at you across darkened clouds
with a spear made from thunder.

What you perceive as my downfall,
will be my rising.

Libby Jenner

Cooling down

I relax in the water,
let it carve my mind like it does the meanders,
and I hear the *tsssk* of steam as the thriving fires
are sent to sleep in the cool ripples.

Fires are ferocious and give me strength,
but the water always brings me back to the present.

My Watery Emotions don't have to be Feared

Weaned on sticky poison
that sealed my throat with a film.
I was a fish out of water:
mouth opening and shutting
desperately
gasping
for
air.

I wonder how many feelings I have had to suppress,
how much of this poison I've swallowed
and lodged my throat with,
to avoid being called
sensitive,
overly emotional,
or dramatic.

This was when I was just a little stream
that with rain would overflow the levees,
but I am now an ocean
that thrashes under thunderous skies
and claws at beaches with colossal waves.

But it is not always flooding and thunder:
sometimes the surface looks as soft as sorbet,
and scoops into my hands just the same,
as I decide whether yesterday's emotions
need to be washed off my face
or whether I need to soak in them.

Libby Jenner

I don't need to keep drowning when my emotions
overflow:
I was built to feel this way.
To reject the current and fear the water
is to fear the change and adaptations I must make.
And now, iridescent scales have emerged over my skin.

I don't think my emotions were ever a threat,
I think I needed the water
to breathe.

Finding an Exit to the Mirror Maze

Being a woman is knowing that I can reclaim what I lost
when the world took away the dolls I played with
and swapped them for thorny roses
that cut the small hands clutching them.

Those scars still burn.

I see myself in the girls that stare a little too harshly
at their reflection,
or when they catch themselves mid laugh
and stare at the floor with blushed cheeks,
I see myself in the girls who hide from a world that offers
too loud a perspective about who they should be.

But being a woman is
learning ways to reclaim what I sacrificed as a child
so that she can rest against my heart
instead of wallowing in my chest.
I feel her hug me
every time I am mesmerised by nature,
every time I wear a colour coordinated outfit,
every time I collect shells,
every time I cackle with happiness,
every time I unashamedly live,
and in these moments, I like to think that
little me breaks free and enjoys them with me.

Maybe she will have the courage
to come away from my heart
and rest permanently behind my smile.

Libby Jenner

Starlight Foresight

Skimming across the waves are reflections of the stars,
and with them are their secrets.
I pull at a strand that glistens close to the shore,
and I see the spiderweb of stars ripple;
I thread them through my hands,
like I'm pulling down fairy lights,
in hopes that some of their wisdom will soak into me.

As each orb of glittering light flows through my hands,
a small hum that, at first,
was too soft to hear against the tumbling waves,
is now tinkling in my ear:
the stars clustered behind me in a mound
are the source of the humming.

Eyes wide, I dive in.

A river of light forms as I submerge,
and I cup my hands into its surface to splash my face with.
As the light trickles from my eye lashes,
I am reunited with the midnight sky and slumbering sea.

What secret did they share?
I cannot tell.
But there's starlight in my eyes, now,
that will guide me through the night.

Wings Unfurled

Anchoring the Past to the Seafloor

The image of who I once was dissolves like sea foam
and the remaining grains of what's left
sink deeper into the water.
She remains embraced by the tendrils of seaweed
that hug her softly,
but with a little restraint,
and the gentle waves erode her harsh edges
so she is soft like the pebbles beneath her.

Though she is part of who I was,
she is better under the waves
where she is no longer in my head with outgrown ideas,
and anxieties that tug at my chest.

In trying to wash her away completely
it only made her voice louder
and riddled with urgency;
but she is muffled where she is anchored.
She can watch me,
and I can acknowledge her.

Because I do want to remember who I once was,
even if we no longer align;
and it gives her a chance
to see who I am becoming.

Libby Jenner

Driftwood

As everyone steps onto their boats
and sails away into their
sunset, dawn, or potentially storm,
I wonder whether I should keep coming back
to this part of the ocean.

When I sailed away,
I came back each year to see their boats pass,
to wave the same waves,
watch as familiarity elapses,
which I thought was comforting.

But each year
I feel a tug in my chest,
a longing,
it pulls me away from this part of the ocean,
and sails me to seas where the current feels different:
where *I* feel different.

This time, as I watch the boats leave,
I know this is my final watch:
this is my silent goodbye.

There is a loneliness
I had not anticipated
when it comes to growing out of spaces
that once felt safe,
and moving on from people
who once felt like home.

And though I am forever grateful

for the lifelong friendships that have grown in new cities,
and the warmth I have created in a home
that I chose for myself,
my heart often thinks of the people on those boats.
And I hope, genuinely,
that there is happiness on their horizons;
and that they sail away from that part of the ocean
where nothing ever changed.

Libby Jenner

Wind Shear

Salty perfume seeps from each toppling wave
as I inhale with the exhales of the wind that
tugs at my chest, unlike anxious pangs but
with surges of inspiration, instead.
May this salty wind carry me through these growing pains
as newness takes its final bow
and is replaced with the next act of unfamiliarity.

Work-Mind balance

I didn't have time for them.
They begged for release weeks ago,
straining my eyes with jelly fish stings
and clogging my throat with watered sobs,
but their holiday request was denied.

I would have allowed them to visit, or
let them travel down my cheeks
and onto my pillow to stay over,
but our schedules clashed,
rotas incompatible.

I didn't want to take the meltdown shift
but they've clocked in, now,
and I can't ignore them for much longer.

So, with an excuse of feeling unwell,
I leave my workplace early
to do unpaid overtime at home
with the guests I've tried to keep away
for weeks.

Libby Jenner

Pain Marks the Spot

Stored in the joints of my limbs,
sealed like a sunken treasure chest,
is agony beyond comprehension.

But this chest is *cursed*.

I must keep it stored:
locked away and contained
in the tension that twists in my stomach,
in the itching that grazes my skin,
in the pain that pulsates through my muscles,
because I cannot let it escape.

There is no treasure in this chest.

It has been
submerged,
swallowed,
drowned,
but I'd rather clog my gills than allow air in.

Until recently…

I want to feel free,
and I never will be
so long as my chest is closed.

So, I crack it open:
and as its contents bleed onto me,
and the murky water subsides,
what is revealed is scarier

Wings Unfurled

than I remember it to be.

Only this time, I feel somewhat stronger
more secure, even
in taking what I buried away, out.

This is no treasure.
I will not be making necklaces from pain;
but it can sit in that chest,
and the lid will stay open
until I work out what to do with it.

This was the condition to feeling content and safe
that I had not contemplated.
Because I am no longer swimming against currents
and my body finally has the space
to process what I buried
all those years ago.

Libby Jenner

Seasick

Nausea ripples in my tightening chest
and my mouth has a foul taste.
I want to get off of this boat
and off this ocean that though
looks calm to the touch,
has whirlpools that beckon me:

Jump in, Jump in, Jump in.

I need something, anything,
to dilute my emotions
so they are less concentrated when swallowed.
I need to remove the tools from my hands
that I've used to hollow my chest
to dig out the rocks that sit
at the base of my stomach.

I drink some water
but it's salty.

I need to get off this boat.
I must jump and let the whirlpools have me;
but instead
I wait
until this boat has drifted me
silently,
quietly,
unseen,
to shore.

Wings Unfurled

Anxiety has a way of chipping me into little pieces
whilst leaving the boat pristine
and the water unrippled.

Libby Jenner

I am here, I always was

I'm under the water
looking at the surface as the light begins to shift.
I follow that last thread of dawning light to the surface
and gasp
as coolness streams into my lungs.

After years of straining my breath, *in case*

> *they realized I was drowning rather than*
> *swimming;*
> *they saw how their boulders of compacted words*
> *anchored me to the floor;*
> *they sensed a change in me that didn't align with*
> *their concocted vision;*

swallowing my shallow breaths was normalised
so I'd barley create noise.

But I don't want to be like that, anymore,
I don't want to be watered down.

I am here!

And though not everyone needs to know it.
I refuse to hide myself in the deep end.

Wings Unfurled

Lake Reflections

As I walk along the outskirts of the lake, I watch as dawn embraces the surface and drapes its soft hues across the thrumming ripples made by paddling ducks. Serenity echoes in the still trees that stand guard along my path, but I veer to the water's edge: dewy grass softens under my steps and my reflection eagerly follows.

I glance down into the water and stumble back.

Peering over the edge, I notice that it is not a woman looking back at me, but a child. A child that shares my autumn eyes, warm hair, and uncontainable smile.

I crouch down as we observe each other, giggling in disbelief, before I stand and continue walking. In my peripheral vision, I see her skip to keep up with me and twirl into the columns of light from the rising sun. Her hair is wild and movements just as; I never remember having a flow that matched both the calm of the lake and the unruly waves of the ocean.

Our thread is cut as I pull away with an enthusiastic goodbye and wavering smile, and I collapse onto the nearest bench by the trees.

And I sob.

She seemed so in awe of me,
and I think I am finally in awe of who we are, too.

Libby Jenner

Wings Unfurled

CHAPTER THREE

I am done burning myself and trying to scorch my being into something that is palatable, submissive, or small. I am creating fires and licking my insecurities with the flames that trickle from my tongue. And from the embers, I will rise again, and again.

But these poems are not just for what I have burnt, but for what I learnt from *being* burnt.

I am a wildfire. And I am learning when to use my fire for destruction and cleansing.

My wings resemble phoenix feathers.

Libby Jenner

A message from the fire butterfly:

Let me give you some kindling for this journey, and perhaps a jar of sparks for when you cannot provide your own. The fire is not there to walk over your skin as you have been walked over, it is for burning a new path for YOU to walk on.

Do not be afraid of the sensuality: embrace its warmth. There is room for seduction amongst the destruction.

Wings Unfurled

Striking Matches and Savoring my Glow

My timeline for healing took a new direction after I learnt how to talk myself back from giving too much of myself to others.

I used to force a smile so bright, it blinded the sun. I built myself to be a beacon for those that needed shelter from their shadows. But some scurried back and forth between me and their darkness: forever hungry for what I could offer but never feeling entirely full.

One day, I had no light left to give. But my sacrifice was not heroic, and it was not kind: I had surrendered my sense of self and I forfeited the kindness that I needed for my own wellbeing to give, give, give, and *give* to everyone around me.

I used to force a smile so bright, it blinded the sun. Now I am content in letting her warm those around me whilst I am merely a gentle hand to hold. When friends need light, I don't sacrifice my own for their expense; I help them strike matches, start fires, bathe in the sun, and soak up the moon. My home is candlelit at night and has extensive bay windows for the sun to trickle through in the day. I allow myself space to rest in it, rejuvenate, glow, and concentrate on my own needs, I compartmentalise my light not for control, but for balance.

I want to give less, and I am happier for it.

Libby Jenner

I have learnt that the way to talk yourself back from giving too much to others is to give that little bit extra you had to yourself.

One Word that Holds a Thousand After-thoughts

I am met with a returning tribulation
that has the power to kill my flame with
its swift disregards and breezy backstabs.
Have I learnt from when I last let someone
suffocate my glow?
Will this candle burn through the night,
leaving it cemented to the table with wax overflow?

With a flicker in my eyes but no falter in my breath,
I respond with:
"no."

The drafty window slams shut,
the hearth ignites,
and this little candle
blushes until daylight.

Libby Jenner

A Love Letter to Poetry

Loving myself feels like writing poetry. Some days the creativity flows from all the sides of my self-portrait, and others it is blocked: I've hit a wall and the concussion radiates into my reflection.

But I remember to tell myself that creativity cannot be forced, so neither should my expectations on how much I can love myself each day.

I accept who I am when I don't like myself, but when I accept who I am when I *do* like myself, it's when I write the best poetry.

Tears Made of Molten Lava

I once knew a girl
with doubt being the feathered threads
that crisscrossed her fragile heart together.

I once new a girl
that grew tired of being called
nice,
sweet,
obedient,
she craved a vivacious fire
that would burn her moulded personality
and leave her new descriptors in the ashes:
Confident.
Emotional.
Powerful.

Now, I know a woman
who emerged from a blazing inferno,
with a smile draped across her tear-stricken face.
And the flare she attaches to her wit
helps her thrive with creative passions.
The flames that once scorched her skin
gently caress her assertive stance,
and glow in the amber dusted embers
of her diffused anger.

I know a woman
whose emotional depth is a sapphire ocean
but she has built her own boats to stay afloat.
Her vulnerability is no weakness, and,
much like broken glass,

Libby Jenner

she is powerful in her pieces,
and more beautiful when the shards
capture the celestial hues of the sun.

I once new a girl,
with trauma in her dewy eyes
who grew into a woman
that saw her potential,
dropped a match,
and watched her empowered self
ignite.

Metamorphosis

I found a match in the dust of debris,
from my last fight with the ghosts of my identity,
and I swallowed it.

It scraped against my chest and ignited my heart,
my skin became radiant from the fires within me,
and I laughed wildly at the darkness
as it cowered in my presence;
its ravenous eyes averted my gaze.

With each laugh I coughed up the shadows that
infested my lungs
and cackled as they were consumed by the flowers
that had begun growing in the cracks of the
broken mirrors that created my solitude:
they asphyxiated their power with pollen filled bites
and spat them out into a pile of compost.

I felt the mirrors shake under the pressure of the flowers
so I rained on the buds,
and trickled light on their unfurling petals,
until the mirrors finally collapsed
and shattered into powder.

I leave a floral tapestry trail behind me
as I stride away from the labyrinth of darkness
that curled itself into a sobbing ball in the embers
of my chrysalis.

Libby Jenner

I have the capacity to give birth,
if I choose it,
and I wish I considered sooner
that I have the capacity to re-birth myself, too.

Fairy Dust from Phoenix Ashes to Initiate my Wildfire

I've conspired against my negative thoughts.
I'm breathing life into the darkness with a lone spark:
a dusting of fire
that licks the ground,
likes the taste,
and waltz's into the looming forest.
And as the embers pulsate on the floor
and enclose my darkness in
a circle of light,
I bend down to its crumpled mess
and laugh with more wildness
than the wildfire I created.

Libby Jenner

Broken Locks on Drafty Windows

I often waver like a flame in the path of a window left ajar,
but there is a quiet strength within me.
Its heartbeat lives within my own,
pulsing courage throughout my bones
so as I stand up
I will never feel alone.

I often waver like a flame in the path of a window left ajar,
but long has it been since my match box was bare,
because even with gusts that threaten my flare
I will always have a little bead of ember left to care for
to provoke what they failed to dampen.

Dolls Questioning The Furnace

though there is so much I could write
about how I have been forced into a furnace
and moulded by harsh hands
to be a figure adored by all to look at,

though there is so much I could write
about my lust for sensuality being sizzled out
by scolding waters that peeled my skin,

though there is so much I could write
about what I have had to unlearn,
in the process of accepting who I am,
and what I am still learning
about how I can live without care for a gaze
that was a magnifying glass in constant search for
'impurities',

though there is so much I could write
about how the patriarchy has scorched into the ground
what a woman should be,

today I want to focus on
not what I should be
but who I am
and who I will be.

Because being a woman is
whatever I want it to be.
But it always feels like the sun.

Libby Jenner

Dolls Breaking The Furnace

Ceramic doll
at the edge
of her case.
She topples

smash

onto the floor.
Fragments cutting
the feet of
those looming
above her
that failed
to see her
F
  A
    L
      L.
Or perhaps
did not care
to intervene.

More porcelain is needed,
but this time to be
moulded with soft,
kind hands,
before being carefully placed
into the kiln to glaze.

Fire licks at her skin and caresses her arms.
The heat warms her as she moves in its presence

Wings Unfurled

and her hands trace every inch of her body:
fond touches, strokes, embraces,
exploration, sensations, succumbing to temptations.

She is drawn out of the kiln.

Solidified in her last stance of indulgence:
one arm raised to the sky, her eyeline following,
the other clutching a bunch of her dress
that is hoisted above her raised thigh.

One bare foot is out in the air,
the other planted on a base of grass as if she is dancing.
Her hair is wild with curling tendrils in a breeze
that we cannot feel.

Fragile, she is, still
but is there not beauty in how no matter
the number of occasions she is   pushed
and left ShAtTeReD in pieces,
chipped by white hands,
she can be built into another version of her ceramic doll
self.

More than a pretty figurine of pristine expectations,
is she, who befriends the feared flames
and lets them melt modifications that were forced upon her
before cooling into a strong figure
of sensual bliss.

Libby Jenner

Shedding my Old Self

I left the shadow of my old self out to dry,
like a floral arrangement tinged brown,
but I didn't want her as a decoration.
I didn't want her at all,
so I burned her.
Lit a match on the person that
spoke too softly
or not at all,
nodded too pleasantly
when she began to fall,
who learnt to repress
before crawl,
who rejected every mirror
to not see just how small
she had made herself.

And as I stared at the ghostly haze of smoke
that swirled around me,
I swear she whispered:
"Thank you."

Wings Unfurled

Active Creativity

My passions have been dormant
but my eruption is impending,
why continue to push down the abundance of
my happiness that is ascending?

My mountain exterior was comfortable,
but there is magma bubbling below
my creativity is rising to the surface
and I am ready for the overflow.

Let this lava carve me a new phase
as the moon changes in its sky,
this alteration has been long anticipated
but with no expectations of what will solidify.

Libby Jenner

I cannot sacrifice myself to save you from this fire

Drip-fed smoke
until I'm coughing up soot
because I didn't walk away from someone else's inferno,
again,
because I thought I could change the outcome,
again,
because I thought getting myself burnt to help others
was the 'right' thing to do,
again.

People-pleasing has left ash on my tongue
and has contributed kindling to a fire
that wasn't even within my reach.
So, with my next chunk of charcoal
that I cough up
I'll draw a confining circle around myself
until my lungs are clean,
my own fire is bright,
and I cannot feel the heat from others
lingering on my temples
and on the back of my neck.

Coven, Community, and Lifeline

I didn't always admire fiery women:
I thought they were something to fear,
until I realised they had never burnt me.
I was just told they would if I got too close.

But what a privilege it is to dance among them,
to feel their warmth,
to glow with them in the moonlight as well as the sun
with adoration and power sewn into our words.
And now I see
why it is they try to isolate us.

But we will not stop adding kindling to our community.
We will not subdue the power we hold.
For it is that exact power that gives us the strength to fight,
and fight we shall,
until they no longer fear our potential
but become inspired by it.

Libby Jenner

Fighting a Bonfire with a sparkler

My skin is too close to the heat
and with it melts
the guards I built around me
that had finally reached the ideal height:
not too tall to cast shadows,
not too small to be stepped over.
But I forgot to fear exposure
when I started burning things;
the enticing flames suffocated the sounds of doubt
that I brushed away like floating pieces of bonfire ash

and
I'm scared.

I'm scared I'll just be left as bones
with a circle of debris around me
and nothing but charcoal to write my next chapter with.

When will I learn when its best to light a match
and when it's safer to stand on dewy grass, instead?

Who I want to be

I want to look at myself and see fire,
strike matches against my skin,
and warm my life with amber flames.

I want to put on a top I wore outside yesterday
and still smell the sunshine
that has soaked into the fabric with a glittering finish.

I want to dress myself in moonbeams,
feel the silky curls hug my skin
and reflect stars in my eyes.

I am done being a droplet of shadow seeking the light.
I want to be flammable.
I want to be sun soaked.
and I want to see nebulas
where I used to see darkness.

Libby Jenner

Wings Unfurled

CHAPTER FOUR

I often float into daydreams and nostalgia: it seems that being above ground is a necessity in my hectic life. The clouds let me rest as I process the changing winds that have knocked me to the ground. With their comfort, I reflect.

There is air in my lungs that needs to be sung, and this voice of mine has only just begun.

My wings are made from clouds.

Libby Jenner

A message from the air butterfly:

The changes that await in your next chapter will never be strong enough to part the clouds that create your wings. They will always drift back to you, and help you soar through the unexpected. And if you ever doubt it, I will be the wind that guides your wings back to you.

I have been the whispers amongst the flowers and the lullabies in the trees, are you ready to listen as I speak directly to you, now?

Though I am but a whisper, do not be afraid to howl. Afterall, my favourite emotional release is a hurricane.

Wings Unfurled

Winds of Change

Autumn has arrived
in decaying woods
and burnt umbers,
and with its arrival is a temperamental friend:

Nostalgia is a train
and I am by the rails.
Do I get on this train?
Do I let it pass me by?
Or do I stand on the tracks?

I go into the toilets,
5 minutes until departure,
my skin sheds onto the floor,
clothes drenched in a musk of expectation,
I dance through this breakdown:
the moves are muscle memory.

After, I peel myself from the floor
and walk,
I walk until the sound of the train
is as faint as the memories it brings.

Nostalgia is like the moon lingering
in rebellion to the sunrise:
out of place, but when it is faded to an etching
you could almost forget it is there.

Libby Jenner

Someone Unveiled Shade onto my Path

I close the gate behind me
as I walk into a current of auburn
that scales each leaf so delicately.
Behind me falls the past,
trapped behind a wooden barrier,
beyond is
serene air speckled with autumn whispers,
clouds like sunken cushions
perched on a bitter breeze,
and a future frosted with promises.
This is my solace of apricot glow
to warm my wintry thoughts.

Balancing the Sun and Moon

When light reached out to me,
for the first time,
I cowered in my abyss
and scurried from the sun
as if it were poison.

                                        an ink stained
                                        landscape.

When light reached out to me,   o
for what could have been   t
the hundredth time,   n
I climbed up a ladder   i
The moon being the guiding hands
to help me escape.

When I realised that the sun
was not the light I needed,
it was too exposing for my gentle frame,
I reveled with the evening and
the stars in her ebony canvas.

I became content with the darkness
when in the presence of moonlight:
content with both parts of my being
that are day
and night.

Libby Jenner

The Secret Language of Flowers

Under their vibrant butterfly hues
is a symphony of unyielding self-love.
Whispers of adoration dance in the wind
and take rest on their pollen dusted beds.

Their love is illustrious,
paints sunsets over grey,
washes doubt with dew.

I thought flowers simply moved in the breeze
but I see them, now,
it's their delicate dance of healing.
If you lay close enough, you can hear the humming
as they relax their nervous systems
and absorb the sun's sweetness,
swallow it down their stems,
before directing it to their roots.
So even if they wilt,
or if they are hurt by trampling feet,
they are still glowing, beneath the surface.

I, too, want to learn this deep-rooted self-love
where my surface is not a priority, as such
but my roots are.

I want to glow from the inside out.

Wings Unfurled

I Traded my Cocoon for a New City

With the vastness of possibilities before me,
I peeled open the glassy folds of my wings,
to let the sun iron out the crinkles,
opened my arms to the wind to
untangle the matted matrix of my being,
coalesced my streams into sea waves
to wash the dried blood from my wounds,
and stood with my toes curled over the edge.

Though time altered my wings,
like splintered spiderwebs on glass,
I eventually adapted to the weathering
by capturing courage in the iridescent scales,
and using glittering threads to close the tears.

Through all I endured,
in this new city I call my home,
I glow at the realization that
unfurling my wings
was most challenging of all:
because when I stood at the edge
of my old world,
I had no idea whether I would fly

or fall.

Libby Jenner

Head in the clouds

Wilting skies from cornflower to lilac
and wispy clouds brushed over its frame,
*why would I ever want to remove my head from this
serenity?*
Why stumble down to the ground
when I am sun-glossed up here?

But then reality tugs
and d
      o
        w
          n
              I go.
Scraping my knees on the fall.

So, I will braid the clouds into my hair,
that sunlight can hang off,
and scatter them like freckles over my skin.
I don't want to lose this imagination
and love for creation
just because I am older.

I crave it, it calls to me,
so I listen
as it sings from the wisps that are woven around my head.
Because I think that this is no child-like wonder
but a romanticised way of living
where awe is constant.

Wings Unfurled

Writer's Fog

Poetry lives in the chambers of my heart
but the ashes of this month have infiltrated,
casting dust over the stanzas.
When the ashes have settled, and swept themselves away,
I won't just have poetry etched against my heart, again,
it will be etched into:

Fairy dust dawns / each tinkering of emotions / a train
going past my window as I'm washing up the day's
stresses / pearlescent strokes of moonlight / the sunflower
warmth of a friend / the lilac underbellies of sunset clouds
/ the first morning smile from my partner/ and…

with each step
I'll plant more words.

Though this month has had a forecast of writer's fog,
I will remember that what I love most about being a poet
is sentamentalising each ounce of my being
and finding the beauty amongst calamity.

Even if the words don't surface,
it is always there,
that soothing melody of poetry,
to remind me that the world is magical.

Libby Jenner

Embracing my Era of Solitude and Hibernation

There's a stillness to mornings that I quite enjoy:
when the breeze is like a lover's hand on my cheek
and my wings rest without the pressure of flying.
Instead, they cradle around my shoulders,
keeping me warm
under the icy guard of the winter sun.
And it is this stillness that I try to go to
when my life feels a surplus of chaos;
it is a stillness I want to follow me
and be anticipating my arrival
wherever I go.

The Raven and The Robin

A raven flew to my lounge window
and perched on the ledge,
it began *tap tap tapping*
and I watched it from the corners of my vision
without lifting my stare from my book
that I was trying my hardest to seem engrossed in.

The following month,
It was back
tap tap tapping
on my bedroom window.
I glanced over this time
to see ebony feathers glazed with sapphire,
but the window remained shut
and I just stared blankly at the bird.

The next month, again,
tap tap tapping
on my kitchen window.
The taps were left running,
from where I was washing up,
as I also ran.
I collapsed in a corner
with my hands clasped over my ears,
and my legs pulled to my ribs.

I didn't see the raven for a few seasons,
until yesterday.

I heard a
tap tap tapping

Libby Jenner

and after noticing the raven, I thought,
Oh, you must be hungry!
So I took a handful of cereal, placed it in a bowl,
and took it outside to my wooden table where
I could be company for its makeshift feast.

After a generous helping, and squawk of gratitude,
I watched as it flew away into the slumbering sky.
My mind was quiet, for a moment,
blissful silence,
just the sky and I,
and then there was a *tap, tap, tapping* in my mind:
I helped the raven.
I went outside.
I wasn't afraid.

And as this catalytic thought began to expand,
I heard a little chirp to my left
and was met with a blushed-bellied robin
also looking for some food.

Wings Unfurled

The Voice out of its Box

When this gift was first presented to me
it was, oddly, when I realised that it had been taken away:
I heard it through a crack in a dusty locked drawer,
and since I was never given a key
I began to smash the wood open.

I am still discovering my voice
and what it is capable of,
I am still learning how to trust it
when it demands to be heard,
and listen to what's around me
when it seeks silence.

But what I am trying not to do
is keep putting her back into
that perfectly packaged box,
of hesitant smiles and uncomfortable laughs,
that gets locked away and forgotten about.

Because my voice should never be taken away
especially of my own doing.

Libby Jenner

Holding Hands Through Time

I hear her across the winds sometimes,
younger me,
as if we are having a long-distance conversation;
and on days where she is fainter,
I call out so she doesn't get lost.

Even though I know she can't really be with me
and I can't show her the life I've made,
which is a repercussion of her choosing to live,
I like to imagine that she is the little surges
of fighting strength within me,
and the words I hear in the wind
on days I am absent.

I like to think
it is her way of showing she loves who she grew into:
and she wants to ensure this version of herself lives, too.

Wings Unfurled

Cloud Formations

Friendships have come in as fast as storm clouds
and separated just as so,
sometimes there are wisps left to grab onto
for a future where our skies align
and our sunsets glow together,
but not always.

Although I used to wish for a blanket of clouds above me
to make me feel warmer and secure,
too many of those clouds blocked out the sun.

So even if there are just a few clouds in my sky,
there will still be a golden sunset
and a rosy dawn,
if they snow
I'll bring my coat,
if they thunder
I'll support their roars,
and if they rain
I'll bring an umbrella
and find a parting for the sun
to cast rainbows against the grey.

Libby Jenner

Cocooned in My Abyss, a dream

I had a dream I was throwing javelins of light
into darkness.
They pierced through the ebony velvet
with scissor-like intricacy
and left amber sear marks in their wake.

Then
a reverberation of impact,
a strong *thud* bounced off the walls of darkness,
echoing a familiar voice across my skin.

I ran towards it.
The closer I got
the colder the air became:
the blankets of darkness now icy shards.

My strides became
trudges
Slow
Slow
e v e r s o s l o w
trudges...

But I was so close to the javelin of light
and something was compelling me
to keep moving:
a small voice, a tiny voice,
muffled...

And there it was,
what I had hit.

Wings Unfurled

I began sinking into the darkness,
unable to kick myself out of the murkiness
or grasp at something to hoist myself out with.
As the darkness consumed me, and I began to waken,
my last look into my dream was an image of
a dark cocoon,
with younger me curled inside
and the javelin buzzing in and out of light at its base.

Libby Jenner

Did the stars write this for me, or will I write for them?

Spoon the star dust into my mouth,
so I have its sheen on my tongue,
and listen as it dusts my speech
with the words of someone created merely
to exist,
to experience,
to live,
it's all the universe wants me to do.

I don't feel as though I owe anyone a purpose
or that I must fulfill a destiny:
there is pressure in feeling you owe the world something,
to offer something of myself to others.

But I think,
the only thing that needs to be fulfilled
should be me:
and I imagine this as a life rich with awe.

What a privilege it is
to be able to start this journey,
to finally feel safe,
in a world which is exasperated by suffering,
in which I have been force-fed my own sharing.

What a privilege is has been so far
to age into adulthood
and, hopefully, continue to do so.

And all of this I can experience
with the stars watching over me

Wings Unfurled

as they wait patiently for me
to come home to them
and return the star dust
that they fed me when
I didn't know who I was,
what I should be doing,
or who I should be.

And I'll return it to them in my final speech:
The Story of My Existence.

Libby Jenner

Wings Unfurled

CHAPTER FIVE

When I need to be grounded, I remind myself that if a plant pot is too small for me, I simply move. I have too much to offer to be contained: I need to be in a meadow.

It is okay that I need to go back to my garden sanctuary if I need to decompress, it is a home for my mind to rest in.

My wings are dewy and growing.

Libby Jenner

A message from the earth butterfly:

Welcome back to your garden, or is this a new plot of land you seek? That is for you to decide.

Nurture all that you are and trim the browning leaves. Let them fall to the soil and decompose: help is not unwanted when burying yourself in healthy soil.

After all, is it not the earth that grew the trees that were made into the first door to your garden? And the peridot door into this next chapter?

And that was grown for you, by you.

What will you grow, next?

Wings Unfurled

Grounded

When I dared to be bold
I found that not everyone liked me.
Not everyone stayed in my circle,
because I was no longer a shape they liked.

But those that stayed
were proud of my growth,
of my confidence,
my new form.

And those that left
liked that my walls crumbled easily,
loved how my fences were flimsy,
and now that you need a key to the gate
they don't like it.

When I dared to be bold
I learnt that it doesn't mean
I can't be gentle, vulnerable, kind:
it means I am all those things,
but not as a service to others.
It's an investment in myself.

Libby Jenner

Seasonal Shifts

Spring is patiently waiting to host,
muttering in yellow,
whispering for daffodils to bloom,
and coaxing the sun to shine brighter.
But I am ready to bloom, too,
so bind me in this warmth and love
to give way for my fluorescence to emanate,
alike to the beauty of a dragonfly's metallic bodice.
May this armor bring aid
as spring propels me in a new direction
where I can leave streams of lacy starlight in my wake.

Wings Unfurled

Safe Space

I've focused so much
on fighting discomfort
that I've forgotten how to make myself
a sacred place to rest
when my old friend, trauma,
claws their way back into the present:
manifesting as a pain that is
untouchable, undetectable, untreatable.

So I will make a sanctuary, perhaps like a greenhouse,
where colour will stream in every corner from glass sun
catchers that scatter rainbows in iridescent beams. Cream
gardenia flowers will adorn the trees and their petals will
cascade delicately onto my lap. As I sit near a trickling
stream, that irrigates the roots of the greenery around me,
I'll let the tranquil music from its journey soothe my mind.
And a bookcase dusted by flickering butterflies will stand
next to a wooden bench where I can sit and escape into a
story.

This sanctuary will be accompanied by soft solitude
so I can bandage my invisible wounds,
and unload my emotions
in tranquillity.

Libby Jenner

I want to be more like Autumn

I have roused from the nightmare
where solace grew like mold in my damp isolation:
I can still remember how thick the air was,
how it crushed me to the floor
and left me with splintered thoughts.

How grateful I am, that I no longer subdue
to a rhetoric that states confinement is where I am safe.
Because, today, I watched as dawn awoke
under the veil of Autumn,
swathing each surface with copper.
Petrichor infused breezes cleared my lungs
of the last pollutants that tugged beneath my rib cage
and my footprints lingered in the fairy dust frost
as I stepped into the tawny glow.

In seasons of doubt, depression, and defeat,
I know I have my autumn changeover awaiting.

Wings Unfurled

Watering Plants

Wilted plants with taupe leaves have been cleared.
Though I watered them,
strengthened their soil,
and gave my light to them,
their wilted character stuck.

Now, I am focusing on the plants
that do not starve me for my energy,
or take advantage of my kind hands,
but thrive in their viridian balayage leaves
as they grow with me.

Libby Jenner

Prioritising Relaxation

My feet are sore,
so I plant them in the cooling dew;
the grass weaves between my toes,
around my ankles,
tendrils of aloe calmness
enticing me to sit down.

Now, as I lay in the grass,
succumbing to the coolness
that oozes over my tense skin,
I feel the Earth diffuse
their nurturing minerals into me
in waves of refreshing thoughts.

Where my body once
ached,
groaned,
bled,
it is now beginning to surrender
to an ameliorating narrative.
Though some scars remain,
I won't be hiding them behind salves
for what an incredible story they tell
that I chose healing
over destruction.

Florets

I want to blossom:
each petal unfurling with elegance,
thorns sharpened with wildness,
stem firm and unfaltering,
and roots strong beneath the weight of her growth.

I want to blossom:
it's a feeling that is always meant to be.
For I am a flourishing flower
of delicacy and ferocity.

Libby Jenner

Music For Growing Flowers

A song you know by heart,
but you've been pouring it into a broken glass.
Yet it dares to live in the ribbons of light
that bounce off the shattered edges.
This is where hope grows:
buds bathe in the slithers of sun
and your vase is soon crowded
with huddled flowers

This song you know by heart,
even though you were never taught it
or potentially shown it,
can be practiced over time
and never has to be earnt.

It's love.
Notes of it flow in you, constantly.
So why pour it into a broken glass
when you can water the vase of flowers,
instead?

On the Other Side of the Mirror

Every time I hate a part of my body
my mirror CrAcKs.
I've noticed that, recently,
flowers are growing between the sharp edges:

Cornflower curls and lilac ripples, powder pink folds with
streaks of yellow dimples, tutu-like petals and fluffy white
dots, dustings of orange and absence of rot.

so,
when I look at those parts of myself I didn't love,
I can see something beautiful bloom.

Now,
when I look into my mirror,
there are no flowers growing.
The mirror is full and smooth,
it always was:
my beauty had fallen into
the cracks of my insecurities
but I now have the energy to retrieve it.

I really am beautiful,
and it radiates from beneath the surface.

Libby Jenner

Flowers Inspire Me

Spring has awoken from her rest
with the softness of tulip petals
and the calm cadence of meandering streams.
She is illustrious with the plethora of buds she entices
with her floral elixir.
And as I walk past the pollen clustered petals
I whisper to myself,
"Love that for them, the same for me."

Frost Flower Meadows

Sometimes I mentally freeze spring,
have the snowflakes coat my hair in chills,
and watch as all that moved is tentatively still.

I walk through the ice with this new time to reflect,
but the earth becomes rigid under my feet
and the bruises signal I am close to defeat.

Reality thaws my last moments to think,
and I must think fast to decide
whether winter is for clarity or a place to hide.

Libby Jenner

The Essence of Spring

Spring is butterfly hues and flowers adorned with gems of dew. Where I unfurl in the sun's embrace and feel my body surge with golden rejuvenation. Flowering buds of auroral colours weave amongst the grass and their scattered shadows dance in the warm breeze. The profound essence of self-love caresses my skin with smells of freshly squeezed clementine juice and floral infusions. Poetry is intimate, delicate, and softer than blushing tulip petals; and I welcome her with awe as she guides my hand across the crinkled pages of my notebook. It's when I run bare foot through my meadow mind with arms outstretched in bliss.

Spring is when I feel ethereal, sensual, liberated.

And it's when I let the wild growth of nature inspire my own.

Evergreen

Skeletal, was my tree
for many years before I learnt how to bloom:
frail branches desperately grabbing at the sun
but broken by a single gust of wind.
How does a tree grow
when it is relentlessly pummeled by lightening?

It doesn't.

Uprooted, fallen, sobbing into the twigs of my existence
and I got comfortable, for some time,
unaware I was becoming part of the ground
that captured my fall.

The soil was rich with kind words, bravery,
I took the last sprouts of my existence
and clutched at them,
I wiggled my torn roots into the words
and watched as they began to glow, mango
like the morning sun,

I have been many trees,
last year I was a willow: calm, serene,
branches swaying like soft ocean waves.
The year before I was an oak: strong, stubborn,
trunk remaining stable during storms.
And this year,
I am a blossom tree: flourishing, gentle,
grateful for vibrance even when fleeting.

Libby Jenner

If I fall,
I believe in myself to grow back, again.
I have hope in the power within kindness,
and the power within myself.

Bouquet

Soft as tulip petals
is my love that is homegrown.
Blushed is my existence
as I bloom alongside them.
And nourished is my soul
as I have learnt to live deliciously.

Libby Jenner

Wings Unfurled

I have learnt so much since I left my garden.
But sometimes I must go back, and that's okay.

"don't be shy, dearest butterfly" was my mantra for the
garden, it coaxed me out of my cocoon.

But now I say,
"Unfurl your wings and soar,
you have too much to experience to be contained;"

Libby Jenner

ACKNOWLEDGEMENTS

To my best friend, thank you for creating such a stunning front cover for my book, yet again. I cannot believe we have been best friends for longer than we haven't, but I also cannot imagine it not being that way. To grow with you through childhood and watch you flourish into your beginning of adulthood has been breath taking: I am in awe of you.

To the love of my life, thank you for eagerly listening to me read the drafts of my poems, motivating me to write, and for all the moments you've supported me when I've faltered in confidence both as a writer and a person. I love you endlessly and always.

To my loved ones, thank you for your genuine excitement about my writing journey, telling me what poems you enjoy, messaging me for book updates, and showing me love that I hope I reciprocate in abundance. I appreciate and adore all of you.

To the poetry pals, I must thank you for giving me the platform and confidence to achieve my writing dreams. I am so grateful for your kindness and encouragement! I wouldn't be able to do it without you.

And to me, thank you. I have really struggled this year, but I have also thrived. And in moments of strain in the future, I can turn to this beautiful book and see that I have strength and creativity within me that will never be lost.

Libby Jenner

ABOUT THE AUTHOR

Libby began writing poetry in secondary school as a therapeutic outlet to regain autonomy of her mind during an intense period of trauma. When she was seventeen, her poetry blossomed from painful retellings to empowering prose, so a year later she decided to create an Instagram account, now known as *libbyjenner.poetry,* to share her words. Her intent was to create an online space where people could be empowered with poetry and feel understood with their mental health struggles.

A repercussion of this was an abundance of support from the poetry community, which encouraged Libby to write her debut poetry and prose book *don't be shy, dearest butterfly* which was released at the start of her third year of university in 2022.

The dawning of *Wings Unfurled* began shortly after this but was paused to complete her dissertation; Libby has since graduated with a Bachelor of Arts degree in Creative Writing.

Now living in Brighton, she has unfurled her own wings in a city that she has made her home, and she hopes to explore more of what she specialised with at University (Women's Writing and Feminist Literature) in her future poetry endeavors.

Libby Jenner